World of Reading

LEVEL 2

THE STORY OF THE GUARDIANS

Written by **Tomas Palacios**

Illustrated by **Ron Lim** *and* **Marcelo Pinto**

Based on the Marvel comic book series **Guardians of the Galaxy**

New York
Los Angeles

marvelkids.com

© 2014 MARVEL

SUSTAINABLE FORESTRY INITIATIVE
Certified Chain of Custody
Promoting Sustainable Forestry
www.sfiprogram.org
SFI-01415
The SFI label applies to the text stock

Printed in the United States of America
First Edition
3 5 7 9 10 8 6 4 2
G658-7729-4-14329
ISBN 978-1-4847-0065-5

This is the story of the
Guardians of the Galaxy!

The Guardians are Super Heroes.
They are Gamora, Star-Lord,
Rocket, Groot, and Drax.

They work as a team
to stop evil aliens.
They protect the cosmos.

Star-Lord is their leader.
He is from planet Earth.

His real name is Peter Quill. He was
a brave kid. He stood up to bullies.

Peter pointed to a shooting star.

His father is from space.

Peter wanted to go find him.

Peter learned about the stars and
planets. He studied very hard.
He went to college for space travel.

Peter trained to become a pilot.
He learned to fly.

Peter built a rocket ship.
He became a space pilot.

It was time for space!
Three, two, one . . . BLAST OFF!
Peter rocketed into the sky.

Peter searched for his dad.

He visited different planets.

He met different aliens.

No one had seen his father.

Peter's last stop was a royal planet.
He searched for his dad there.

A man learned of Peter's arrival.
He went to see Peter.
It was Peter's father!

Peter talked to his dad.
He learned there were evil aliens in
space. They wanted to hurt Earth.

Peter wanted to stop them.
Peter could not do it alone.

His father gave Peter a gift.

It was a ship called the *Milano*.

He also gave Peter a suit.
It gave him special powers.

Peter put on the suit.
He became Star-Lord!
He could run faster. He became
stronger. He could even fly!

Star-Lord searched for a special
team. He looked for Super Heroes
just like him.

He met Drax, Groot, Rocket, and Gamora. They would help Star-Lord fight the evil aliens. They would protect the cosmos.

The aliens were coming.

They were going to invade Earth!

There were many of them!

The aliens flew from their ship.
They got ready for battle.
They flew toward the Guardians!

The Guardians flew from the *Milano*.
They got ready for battle as well!
They flew toward the aliens!

The Guardians clashed with the
aliens. There was a big space fight!

There were many aliens.
Would the Guardians win?

The Guardians were in trouble!
Groot was hurt. The aliens used
weapons that were very strong.

Rocket had stronger weapons.
Rocket protected his friend. So
did Gamora, Drax, and Star-Lord.
They worked as a team.

A ship fired a big laser at the Guardians! It was Groot's turn to fight! Groot grew big and protected his teammates.

The aliens were losing and retreated!
The Guardians defeated the aliens!
They saved the day!

Sometimes evil will look for a fight.
The Guardians of the Galaxy will
be there to stop them!